P9-DLZ-905

"Alex! You haven't told your mom about spending that money at the carnival?" Janie exclaimed. "Does that mean you don't have any lunch money?"

"Yep."

"What are you going to do at lunchtime?"

Alex shrugged. "Just not eat, I guess."

"But, Alex, you have to eat lunch!" Janie cried. "They don't let kids sit in the cafeteria and not eat anything."

Alex's eyes opened wider and wider as she realized Janie was right. "I'll have to hide somewhere."

Peanut Butter and Jelly Secrets

Nancy Simpson Levene

Chariot Books is an imprint of Chariot Victor Publishing,
a division of Cook Communications, Colorado Springs, Colorado 80918
Cook Communications, Paris, Ontario
Kingsway Communications, Eastbourne, England

PEANUT BUTTER AND JELLY SECRETS
© 1987 by Nancy S. Levene for text and GraphCom Corporation for interior illustrations

All rights reserved. Except for brief excerpts for review purposes, no part of this book may be reproduced or used in any form without written permission from the publisher.
Cover design by Bill Paetzold
Cover illustration by Neal Hughes

First printing, 1987
Printed in the United States of America
00 99 98 97 16 15

Library of Congress Cataloging-in-Publication Data
Levene, Nancy S., 1949-
Peanut butter and jelly secrets.
Summary: After spending her school lunch money at a carnival and trying to hide the fact that she is skipping lunch every day, Alex decides that disobeying her parents causes too many problems.
[1. Obedience—Fiction. 2. Conduct of life—Fiction]
I. Dorenkamp, Michelle, ill. II. Title.
PZ7.L5724Pe 1987
[Fic]

87-5247

ISBN 1-55513-303-7

To my Shepherd
who opens the gate and
leads me forth
and
To Maribeth Land
who grasps His hand and
journeys through victorious
valleys.

The Lord is good and glad to teach the proper path to all who go astray; he will teach the ways that are right and best to those who humbly turn to him. And when we obey him, every path he guides us on is fragrant with his lovingkindness and his truth.

Psalm 25:8-10
The Living Bible

ACKNOWLEDGMENTS

Thank you Ed, Lindsay, Ann, and Jeanne for your prayers and encouragement.

Thank you Vicki, Karen, and Lisa for many word processing hours.

Thank you, Cara, for being my biggest encourager and for laughing, crying, joking, worrying, praising, learning, teaching, and sharing your whole self with Alex and me.

CONTENTS

1 A Five-Dollar Mistake 9
2 The Goblin Strikes 22
3 A Dark Hideout 34
4 Midnight Sneak 45
5 Treasure Hunting 56
6 The Valley of the Shadow of Death 66
7 Crash! Crash! Smash! Shatter! 75
8 Listen to My Heart 85
9 Caught at Last 95
10 Higher Up the Mountain 105

The ALEX Series

by Nancy Simpson Levene

- Shoelaces and Brussels Sprouts
- French Fry Forgiveness
- Hot Chocolate Friendship
- Peanut Butter and Jelly Secrets
- Mint Chocolate Miracles
- Cherry Cola Champions
- The Salty Scarecrow Solution
- Peach Pit Popularity
- T-Bone Trouble
- Grapefruit Basket Upset

CHAPTER 1

A Five-Dollar Mistake

"Mom! Janie says her mother can take us to the school carnival," Alex cried, dangling the telephone receiver by its cord.

"I want to go!" shouted a voice from the floor. Alex looked down. Her six-year-old brother, Rudy, was wrestling with their puppy, T-Bone.

"Now, Rudy, we have talked about this before," Mother said firmly. "You cannot go because you have had a bad cold this past week and I think you should stay home."

"It's not fair!" Rudy hollered and stomped from the room.

"Mom! Janie's waiting on the telephone. Can I go?" Alex danced around in a circle, twisting the telephone chord around her waist.

"Yes, I think that would be all right," answered her mother.

"YIPPEE!" Alex shouted. She started to tell Janie the good news, but she was so tangled in the telephone cord that she couldn't get the receiver up to her ear.

"Oh, Alex, for heaven's sake!" Mother laughed. She twisted and turned Alex around and around until Alex was free from the cord.

"I'm supposed to be at Janie's in fifteen minutes," Alex announced, hanging up the phone.

"Okay, Honey," her mother replied. "Comb your hair and have a good time."

"Mom, I don't need to comb my hair to have a good time."

"Comb it anyway, Alex," Mother laughed.

Alex grumbled but started upstairs to obey. She stopped suddenly. "Mom, I need money!" she shouted.

Mother hurried to the bottom of the stairs. "Alex, all I have is a ten-dollar bill. It's on top of my dresser. You can take it, but I want you only to spend half of it at the carnival. The other half is for your school lunch money next week. Do you understand?"

"Sure, Mom," Alex clattered up the rest of the steps.

"Alex!" called Mother. "Remember, five dollars is all you can spend."

"Brussels sprouts, Mom, I know what half of ten dollars is."

"I'm just making sure you understand," answered her mother.

Alex swooped a comb through her hair, jumped back down the stairs three steps at a time, and banged out the back door. She headed for the gate in the fence that separated her backyard from Janie's backyard.

Janie and Alex were best friends. Janie was not exactly like Alex and Alex was not exactly like Janie, but they were still best friends. Alex liked to climb things, like fences and trees and tall dirt piles. Janie would rather dress up in her mother's old clothes or bake a batch of cookies. Alex loved sports. She was on a softball team and a swimming team. Janie loved to dance. She took ballet and modern dance lessons. Yet, in spite of their differences, the girls loved to be with each other. They did things that they liked to do together—

like roller skating or bike riding or spending the night at each other's house. And sometimes Alex would play dress-up with Janie, and sometimes Janie would play softball with Alex.

"Alex! Are you ready?" Janie called from her back door. Alex ran the rest of the way to Janie's house and the two girls hopped in the car.

"Girls," said Janie's mother as they pulled into the school parking lot. "I will show you the booth in which I will be working. I want you to check in with me every hour so that I know you are all right."

"Okay," the girls agreed. They followed Janie's mother to her booth. It was called the Barrel Toss. Each child got three chances to throw a ball into a barrel. If the ball landed in the barrel, the child won a prize.

"Hey, I bet I can do this easy," cried Alex. She stood behind the line, swung her right arm in two circles, and let go of the ball. BAM! It plopped right into the barrel. So did ball two and ball three.

"Where's my prize?" Alex grinned.

Janie's mother laughed. "Alex, I don't think

we should let you play this game. You are too good. By the way, you have to give me a ticket before you can get a prize."

Alex ran to the ticket counter and bought a string of tickets. So did Janie. Alex gave one ticket to Janie's mother and received a pink bracelet as a prize. Janie's mother laughed at the disappointed look on Alex's face. She took back the bracelet and handed Alex a package with a ball and jacks inside.

"That's better," Alex told her.

"Okay, you two, scram, so I can set up my booth," ordered Janie's mother. "Have a good time and check in with me in an hour."

Alex and Janie scurried away. They stopped at a cotton candy stand and bought bright pink balls of the fluffy candy. Then they began their trip around the carnival, stopping to play the games that interested them.

Everywhere they went, they heard reports about the spooky haunted house set up in the basement.

"I don't think I want to go to the haunted house, Alex," said Janie after listening to someone tell about a gigantic mummy that greeted each visitor.

"Well," Alex replied. "I know my mom wouldn't want me to go. She doesn't even want us to watch scary movies."

The girls were standing in front of the Cake Walk room. "Let's try and win a cake," Janie suggested. She and Alex joined a group of people who were circling the room, stepping on numbers taped to the floor. Whenever the music stopped, a man called out a number. If someone was standing on the number he called, that person won a cake.

After three tries, Alex's number was called. She chose a chocolate cake with chocolate icing.

"Alex, that's neat!" Janie shouted. "Let's take it to my mom so she can keep it for you."

On the way back to the Barrel Toss, the girls spied two boys from their class.

"Uh, oh, Eddie Thompson and Allen Jacobs," whispered Alex. "Quick, don't let them see us."

But it was too late. "Whirlywind, where'd you steal that cake from?" Eddie hollered. He called Alex "Whirlywind" because of her fast pitching arm. Alex could pitch a softball better than any of the boys in her class.

"Better put that cake back," cried Allen in a loud voice. "You know it's not nice to steal!"

"She didn't steal it! She won it!" Janie shouted at the boys.

"Just go away," Alex told them. She kept on walking. Eddie and Allen were always causing trouble. She had learned that it was best to try and ignore them.

"Whirlywind, have you been to the haunted house yet?" called Eddie.

"Aw, I bet they are too scared to go," jeered Allen.

"We are not scared to go to the dumb old haunted house," Alex shouted at Eddie and Allen. "We just don't want to!"

"Chicken, chicken, chicken," the boys sang. They ran off making clucking noises.

"Ooooooh, they burn me up!" Janie stamped her foot.

After delivering the cake to Janie's mother, Alex surprised Janie by saying, "You know, maybe we really ought to try the haunted house."

"What?"

"Well, I was thinking. What if we are the only ones in our class that didn't go to the haunted house? I mean, everyone will think we were scaredy cats."

"Oh."

"Let's just go see what it's like," Alex urged. "We can leave if we want to."

"Okay," Janie said slowly. "I'll do it for you, but not for anybody else."

The girls ran down a hall to a stairway. At the top of the stairs was a sign that read, "THIS WAY TO THE HAUNTED HOUSE. ENTER AT YOUR OWN RISK."

"How much is it?" Alex asked a lady who was selling tickets.

"Fifty cents," the lady replied.

"Fifty cents! Alex, I only have a quarter left," Janie moaned.

Alex pulled her money out of her pocket. She had a five-dollar bill and three quarters. "My mom told me not to spend the five dollars, but with your quarter and my three quarters we can get in," she told Janie.

The girls handed the lady their quarters and followed the line of people down the stairs. About halfway down, the stairway disappeared. In its place was a giant slide. Alex peered down the slide. She could not see the bottom.

"I'll go first," she said bravely.

"Alex, I don't know about this," Janie whispered nervously.

"Janie, it'll be okay. We can go down together. Get on the slide behind me."

The two girls climbed onto the steep slide. They immediately plunged into a dark tunnel.

"Ahhhhhhh!" Janie screamed in Alex's ear.

Alex squinted through the darkness. She was suddenly filled with terror when she saw a ghostly form waiting for them at the bottom of the slide—the mummy!

Alex hardly ever screamed. But this time she did. It was hard to tell who screamed the loudest—Alex or Janie.

The girls hit bottom and landed on something soft and squishy. Alex could not keep her balance. She tried to stand up but fell back against Janie. The mummy bent over them. There were no eyes in its face, only dark holes where its eyes should have been. A loud horrible laugh came from deep in its throat.

Alex was terrified but somehow managed to pull herself to her feet. She grabbed Janie's arm and dragged her friend away from the mummy. The girls stumbled around a corner and BANG! They collided with a skeleton. Alex shrieked. Janie cried. Behind the skeleton, lying on the floor, was what looked like a dead body. Alex stared at it, fully expecting it to rise up and chase her. It did not move but the fear that it would move was awful.

Janie began sobbing hysterically. Alex moved herself and Janie slowly around the "body."

"RUN!" Alex cried.

Janie ran! She ran blindly, covering her face with her hands. Alex held onto Janie and steered them through the darkened maze. They raced past one horrible figure after another.

"GET OUT! GET OUT!" Alex's mind screamed. It was her only thought—to get out of there as fast as she could.

Finally, Alex glimpsed the EXIT sign. She

made for it but suddenly a ghost blocked the way. Alex, still clutching Janie, charged full speed into the ghost, knocking it back against a wall. "Ugh," came a muffled protest from the ghost. The girls ran through a doorway, up some stairs, down a hallway, and into the brightly lit gymnasium. They collapsed on the floor of the gym.

It was several minutes before either of them could speak. Then Alex announced, "I am never going into a haunted house again!"

Janie nodded. Her eyes were red from crying and her face was streaked with tears.

"I'm sorry, Janie, for taking you in there," Alex apologized.

"That's okay," Janie murmured. "At least now we can say we went to the haunted house," she added a little more brightly.

"Brussels sprouts," was all Alex replied.

"I'm thirsty," Janie said after a moment.

"Me, too," agreed Alex, "but we are out of money."

"Yeah," Janie sighed. "I wish we hadn't spent it on the haunted house. I'd like to try the Cake Walk again. Maybe I could win a cake this time."

Alex didn't say anything. She was thinking about the extra five dollars in her pocket—the money that her mother had told her not to spend. She was thinking about spending it anyway. After all, it was her fault that they were out of money. She had talked Janie into spending her last quarter on the haunted house. And her friend had been so scared. Maybe she could make it up to Janie by sharing the five dollars with her. Besides, what fun was a carnival without money?

"Aw, why not," Alex decided. She pulled the

five-dollar bill out of her pocket. "Let's get something to drink and eat. I'm starved."

Janie's eyes brightened. She followed Alex to the drink counter and then to the hot dog stand.

"I hope your mom doesn't get too mad when she finds out you spent the five dollars," Janie told Alex.

"Let's don't think about it now," replied Alex. "Come on, let's go to the Cake Walk."

CHAPTER 2

The Goblin Strikes

When Alex got home, her mother asked, ''Did you have a good time at the carnival?''

''Sure,'' Alex answered, ''it was great—except for the haunted house.''

''The haunted house?''

''Yeah, I sorta talked Janie into going in it, and now I wish I hadn't.''

''Was it pretty bad?'' Mother asked.

''Really bad,'' Alex sighed. She told her mother about the mummy, the skeleton, the dead body, and the ghost that she knocked against the wall on the way out.

''Well, that's one way to get rid of a ghost,'' Mother chuckled.

''I don't understand it,'' Alex complained. ''I didn't like the haunted house at all. Other kids liked it. Why didn't I?"

"Maybe it all seemed too real to you," Mother suggested.

"Yeah," Alex agreed. "Even though I knew they were only people dressed in costumes, they were really spooky."

Mother smiled. "I am sure I would have felt the same way. You see, Alex, I think that because we are Christians, we don't like to be around anything that seems evil—even pretend evil. The next time you feel scared, you might try saying a prayer. You will be surprised at how much that helps." Mother gave Alex a pat on the head, then looked at her face closely.

"I think you need to wash your hands and face. It looks like everything you ate at the carnival is still on your face. Did you save five dollars as I asked you to?"

Alex did not answer her mother because at that moment an arrow whizzed past her nose! It hit the refrigerator and stuck. Alex and Mother stared, openmouthed, at the arrow vibrating up and down on the side of the refrigerator. "Rudy!" they yelled.

A frightened face, smeared with bright-colored paint, peeked around the corner.

"Rudy! Come here this instant!" Mother demanded.

Alex watched her younger brother shuffle slowly into the kitchen. Rudy was not his real name. His real name was David, but he had called himself "Rudy" for as long as Alex could remember. Everyone called him "Rudy," except Alex. She usually called him "Goblin."

If her mother hadn't been so angry, Alex would have laughed out loud. Rudy's once blond hair was now streaked with blue, orange, green, and crimson color. It stuck straight up through a headband holding feathers that drooped to his chin. Globs of paint splotched his T-shirt and blue jeans. He clutched his bow and arrows behind his back.

"Rudy! I have told you many times not to shoot arrows in the house," cried Mother. "Don't you realize how dangerous it is to shoot arrows at people? Even the arrows with rubber tips? I don't ever want to see you do that again!"

Mother was furious. She took the bow and

arrows from Rudy and said, "You need to learn to obey your parents, Rudy. Right now I'm too angry to decide your punishment. I want you to go upstairs. You'll have to take a bath and wash your hair. What is that stuff in your hair and on your face?"

Rudy hesitated, but finally said in a low voice, "Barbara's paint."

"Uh, oh!" Alex gasped. Their older sister, Barbara, was drawing a world map for a special school project. She had been working on it for two weeks.

"Barbara's poster paint?" Mother exclaimed. A horrified look crossed Mother's face. She grabbed Rudy by the arm and marched upstairs to Barbara's bedroom. Alex followed. There, on a desk, was the almost finished poster. Drops of fresh paint were now splattered over one corner of the map. To Alex it looked as if the sky above Alaska had multicolored chicken pox.

"You are in double trouble!" Mother told Rudy. She swatted his bottom. Rudy howled his way to his bedroom.

Alex tiptoed to her own bedroom. It was best to stay out of the way of an angry mother. She was glad that it was her brother who was in trouble and not herself. She hadn't done anything wrong. Or had she? Hadn't she just spent five dollars at the carnival that she wasn't supposed to have spent? Brussels sprouts! She had disobeyed her mother, too!

"Better not tell Mom about the money right now," she told herself. "Better wait until she's in a good mood."

Alex stayed in her room until almost dinnertime. She heard her sister scream when the ruined map was discovered.

"You could always make those colors into a rainbow," suggested Alex as she entered Barbara's bedroom. "It'd be sort of pretty to have a rainbow over Alaska."

Her sister didn't answer. She just stood over the map and glared at it. Alex left the room. "I guess Miss Mushy doesn't want to talk about rainbows right now," Alex decided.

Alex called her sister "Miss Mushy" because her sister liked to dress up in pretty dresses, curl her hair into different styles, sunbathe for hours in the hot sun, and paint her fingernails different shades of color—all things that Alex thought were dumb or boring.

"Oh, well," Alex told herself. "Miss Mushy probably wouldn't like the rainbow idea anyway. She never likes my ideas. Just because she's almost thirteen and I'm only nine, she thinks I'm a dumb little kid!"

That evening at dinner, when Alex's father asked her about the carnival, Alex quickly changed the subject. She did not want to talk about it because she did not want her mother to remember the five dollars she was supposed to have saved for lunch money. No one asked her about the haunted house. Her family's thoughts turned to Barbara's poster.

"What can I do?" Barbara wailed. "I have to turn in the map to my teacher on Tuesday. I can't possibly do it all over again. It took me a week to draw and another week to label all the countries and cities and rivers and oceans!" She hid her face in her hands.

"You're right," agreed Father. "Tomorrow's Sunday. That doesn't give you much time." He reached over and patted Barbara's arm.

"There must be something you can do to fix it," said Mother.

"It's ruined!" Barbara moaned. "Ruined!" She slapped the table with her hand and glared at Rudy. "It's all your fault!"

Rudy stared at his toes and didn't answer.

"Maybe you could cover up the splotchy part with white paint and then draw in the top part of Alaska again," suggested Mother.

"I couldn't get it to match," complained Barbara. "My teacher would think that I goofed!"

"I told her she ought to make it into a rainbow," Alex told her parents.

"A rainbow?" smiled Mother.

"Oh, brother," Barbara scowled.

"Wait a minute! That's it!" shouted Father.

"It is?" asked Alex, Mother, and Barbara.

"Sure! You've heard of the northern lights over Alaska, haven't you?" Father asked them.

"What's that got to do with a rainbow?" Barbara frowned.

"Nothing, really," Father admitted. "The rainbow idea made me think of them." He smiled at his older daughter. "I think you might be able to turn the paint drops into beautiful northern lights. After all, you are the artist of the family."

"Hmmm" considered Barbara. The frown slowly left her face as she thought more and more about the idea.

Father glanced at Alex with a twinkle in his eye. Alex was thrilled to think that one of her ideas might help to solve an important problem. They watched Barbara's face anxiously.

"What color are the northern lights?" Barbara asked her father.

“I think they’re a greenish color,” he replied.

“I thought they were pink or red,” Mother disagreed.

“I’m not sure,” reflected Father. He turned to Barbara. “You’ll have to look them up in the encyclopedia.”

The next day, Barbara worked on her map. She informed her parents that they were both right about the color of the northern lights. The encyclopedia said that they were usually green, but when the lights were especially strong, they had a reddish color.

Alex paid no further attention to the map. She and Janie were busy designing a playhouse. They hoped their fathers would build it for them. Rudy was grounded. Mother said she was the one who was really being punished, because she was stuck inside with Rudy all day.

On Monday morning, Alex’s mother reminded her to take her lunch money to school. She didn’t ask Alex if she had the money. She just reminded her to take it.

While walking to school with Janie, Alex felt uneasy. She hadn’t said that she had her lunch money—so she hadn't actually told her mother a lie. Still, by not answering her mother, Alex had let her mother think that she had her lunch money.

"Brussels sprouts!" Alex yelled out loud.

Janie jumped at the outburst. "What's the matter?" she asked Alex.

"Oh, I'm just getting mixed up," sighed Alex. "I mean, I guess I should tell Mom about us spending all that money at the carnival, except then I'll get in trouble."

"I forgot all about that!" Janie exclaimed. "You mean you haven't told your mom yet?"

"No," Alex sighed.

"Alex?" Janie suddenly stopped and stared at her friend. "Does that mean you don't have any lunch money today?"

"Yep."

"What are you going to do at lunchtime?"

Alex shrugged her shoulders. "Just not eat, I guess."

"But, Alex, you have to eat lunch!" Janie cried. "They don't just let kids sit in the cafeteria and not eat anything. Mrs. Tuttle would be worried and call your mom or something!"

Alex's eyes opened wider and wider as she slowly realized that Janie was right. Her teacher would not let her go without eating lunch. What was she going to do?"

"I'll have to hide somewhere," decided Alex.

"What?" Janie shouted. "Alex, where could you hide?"

"I don't know but I'll think of someplace," Alex answered.

"I don't think it's going to work, Alex," Janie warned. "I think you're going to get in trouble!"

All morning long, Alex worried about lunchtime. What was she going to do? Where could she hide? She couldn't stay behind in the classroom. Mrs. Tuttle surely would notice if she didn't line up and follow everybody down the hall. What could she do?

By the time Mrs. Tuttle called everyone to line up for their march to the cafeteria, Alex still had not thought of a good hiding place. She let everyone else get in line and then she shuffled to the end of it. Her heart was pounding. She knew she had to find somewhere to hide before she reached the cafeteria.

As the class moved down the hallway, Alex lagged further and further behind. She frantically considered every door she passed. *The library? No, the librarian would see me. The nurse's office? No, I'd have to say I was sick, and she'd call my mom. Hey! Wait a minute! I know!*

Quick as a wink, Alex opened a door, stepped inside, and closed it as quietly as she could. She leaned against the closed door and waited until she could no longer hear footsteps. Finally, the only thing she could hear was her own rapid breathing and thumping heart.

Alex sank to the floor. "Now, I've really done it," she told herself. "If Mrs. Tuttle catches me in the janitor's closet, I've had it! Brussels sprouts!"

CHAPTER 3

A Dark Hideout

It was dark in the janitor's closet—so dark that all Alex could see were tiny cracks of light around the door edges. She sat on the floor, her back against the door, staring into the blackness of the closet.

"Don't be scared!" she whispered to herself. "There's nothing in here 'cept a bunch of rags and mops and brooms and stuff like that."

Still, it was awfully dark, and Alex kept thinking about the haunted house with its terrifying mummy, skeleton, dead body, and ghost. But she also remembered her mother's suggestion to say a prayer whenever she was afraid. "I'll say something from the Bible," Alex decided.

She thought of all the Bible verses she knew. She couldn't remember any about being shut in a dark closet. There was, of course, the 23rd Psalm. Alex had memorized it when she was only five years old. She knew it was a good psalm to say whenever she was afraid or in trouble, but there was a particular part of that psalm that frightened her. It was the part about walking "through the valley of the shadow of death." Many times she had tried to imagine what the valley of the shadow of death might be. She shivered every time she thought about it.

But Alex could think of no other Bible verse to say. She took a deep breath and recited Psalm 23 in a loud whisper:

> The Lord is my shepherd; I shall not want. He maketh me to lie down in green pastures: he leadeth me beside the still waters. He restoreth my soul: he leadeth me in the paths of righteousness for his name's sake. Yea, though I walk through the valley of the shadow of death, I will fear no evil: for thou art with me; thy rod and thy staff they comfort me. Thou preparest a table before me in the presence of mine enemies:

> thou anointest my head with oil; my cup runneth over. Surely goodness and mercy shall follow me all the days of my life: and I will dwell in the house of the Lord for ever.

Alex sighed. Even though she didn't understand it, the psalm had made her feel better.

Suddenly a loud ringing noise shattered the silence of the closet. Alex jumped to her feet. For a moment she thought the whole closet might explode from the sound! What was it?

After a few seconds, Alex realized that that noise was the same school bell that rang many times during a day. Somehow it sounded different and a lot louder from inside the janitor's closet. That ring meant that the third and fourth graders' lunch period was over and it was time for recess. Alex wondered how she was going to be able to get back in line with her classmates without Mrs. Tuttle seeing her.

She opened the door of the closet a tiny crack—just enough to peek out into the hallway. She could hear footsteps—many footsteps—coming her way.

Children and teachers began to pass by her door. Suddenly, Alex saw Janie. She longed to cry out to her friend but she didn't dare.

All of a sudden, a figure blocked the crack through which Alex was peeking. Mrs. Tuttle! Alex didn't breathe. Her hand on the doorknob shook so much that she was afraid it might rattle the door!

Mrs. Tuttle stood in front of the janitor's closet for several seconds. Why had her teacher stopped? Had Mrs. Tuttle somehow seen her?

Her teacher motioned for the children in line to hurry up. She then continued to lead them down the hall. Alex watched her classmates, one by one, pass by the crack.

Alex let out a big gasp of air. That was close! Now came the hard part. Somehow, she had to get to the end of the line without anyone seeing her. She would wait until the last child in line passed her and then she would sneak behind that person. She had to be quick!

Soon, Alex saw her chance and sneaked rapidly out of the closet. She began to march right behind Lorraine, the last person in line.

Alex's blood pounded in her head. She felt hot and shaky, but she kept marching. Lorraine gave Alex several surprised and confused backward glances.

The line of children moved through the outside doors and onto the playground. As Alex passed Mrs. Tuttle at the door, she was almost sure that her teacher looked at her in a funny way.

Alex kept marching out the door and all the way to the far fence of the playground. She noticed Janie and several other friends following her, but she didn't stop until she reached the fence. Only then did she feel she could breathe again.

"ALEX!" Janie ran up to her friend. "You weren't at lunch! Did you hide somewhere?" Janie looked almost as worried as Alex felt. Alex quickly told her and the other girls about her adventure in the janitor's closet.

"Here," Janie dug in her pocket, "I saved you some crackers. It was all I could get."

Alex took the package of crumbled crackers from Janie and smiled. It was just like Janie to think of her friend being hungry. Alex was so

grateful and so glad to see her friend again that she did something unusual. She gave Janie a great big hug!

When Alex got home from school, she had a headache. She hardly ever got headaches—just when she was sick. She also felt tired and dizzy. She was sure it was from skipping lunch. All she'd had to eat since breakfast was a package of crackers. The thought of missing all of her lunches this week was awful. What could she do? Alex was too hungry to think. Would dinner never come?

Suddenly a joyful shout came from her sister's bedroom. Alex ran across the hall and into Barbara's room.

"HURRAY! I JUST FINISHED IT!" Barbara cried. "Well, what do you think?" she asked Alex, holding her world map up for Alex to see.

"Brussels sprouts," gasped Alex. She could no longer see the multicolored chicken pox that had been there before. In its place a greenish glow appeared. Above the glow, brilliant green bands of color arched across the sky over Alaska and Canada. Beams of light shot upward through the bands toward the middle of the sky.

The longer Alex stared at the map, the more the beams seemed to flash and sparkle, almost as if they were moving. How had Miss Mushy done it?

"Amazing!" whispered Alex. She turned to her sister. "Mom's right. You should be an artist when you grow up."

"Think so?" grinned Barbara. "I think it turned out pretty good, myself." She put an arm across Alex's shoulder. "Thanks for the idea, Squirt."

Just then Mother called, "DINNER!"

"Finally!" Alex shouted. She raced downstairs to the dining room and was the first to plop into a chair.

Alex ate everything on her plate and asked for more. She didn't even complain about eating coleslaw.

"Well, Firecracker," her father commented after her second helping, "it looks like you have a bottomless pit!" Father was always cracking goofy jokes. He called Alex "Firecracker." He had nicknames for Barbara and Rudy, too. He called Barbara "Princess" and Rudy "Steamroller."

Alex grinned at her father. She was feeling much better now. She grabbed a drumstick off the chicken platter and announced, "One more piece for the pit!"

Her mother rolled her eyes at Alex. "Didn't you eat very much at lunch today, Alex?" she asked.

"Lunch!" Barbara interrupted. "I almost forgot! I need to take a sack lunch tomorrow. We're going on a field trip."

As the rest of the family discussed Barbara's field trip, an idea came to Alex. "That's it!" she told herself. "I can take a lunch to school tomorrow, and I won't have to sit in the janitor's closet. I'll have to be real sneaky and make it when nobody's looking since Mom doesn't like us to take our lunches. She thinks we get better stuff to eat at school—like yucky vegetables."

After dinner, Alex waited for Mother to finish cleaning in the kitchen. But as soon as Mother left the kitchen, Barbara began making her lunch to take on the field trip. By the time her sister was finished, it was time for Alex to get ready for bed. She still hadn't been able to make a lunch for tomorrow.

"Oh, well, guess it's the janitor's closet again," Alex sighed. As she got into bed, her eyes caught sight of her clock radio sitting on a table by the bed. She could set her alarm for the middle of the night and, while everyone else was asleep, make a secret lunch!

Alex sat up in bed and reached for her clock radio. She held down the button that changed the alarm. It was fun to watch the numbers whiz by. When the numbers said *12,* she let up on the button. That would be midnight! Surely her family would all be asleep at midnight.

Alex lay down again. It was exciting to think of a secret journey at midnight. Alex had a hard time going to sleep. When she finally did fall asleep, she had the strangest dream. She was running through a beautiful green meadow when suddenly Mrs. Tuttle popped out from behind a rock and told her to get in line. She tried and tried to find the end of the line, but every time she thought she'd found it, another child would appear. There seemed to be no end to the children and no end to the line! A noisy school bell kept ringing through her dream. It hurt her ears.

Suddenly, Alex awoke. That wasn't a school bell. That was her alarm. It was midnight!

CHAPTER 4

Midnight Sneak

Alex fumbled for her radio and shut off the alarm. Her ears continued to ring from the noise. Her bleary eyes squinted at the clock. Midnight!

She sat still for a long time and listened. She had to be sure that no one else had been awakened by the alarm. She could hear nothing from the other bedrooms except her father's snoring.

Alex silently crept to the top of the stairs and looked down. The first few steps were softly lit by the hallway night-light, but the bottom part of the stairs was pitch black!

"You have to go down there," Alex told herself. "You can turn on a light when you get downstairs." Forcing herself to be brave, Alex sneaked down one step at a time. "Brussels sprouts, these steps are squeaky.'' Funny, she didn't remember them being so squeaky in the daytime. With every squeak, Alex stopped, afraid that her parents might hear her. ''Shhhhh!'' she whispered to each step.

When she was almost to the bottom, Alex peered over the railing. Dim light from outside shone through the living room windows, casting eerie shadows all over the room. Alex took a deep breath, hurried down the rest of the steps, ran to the nearest lamp, and switched it on. Instantly, the shadows disappeared.

Snapping on lights as she went, Alex rushed to the kitchen. She jerked an apple and the grape jelly jar from the refrigerator. She dug the bread out of the bread box and grabbed the peanut butter off a shelf. Working furiously, Alex slapped together two peanut butter and jelly sandwiches and fitted them into sandwich bags. She quickly rinsed off the apple and dried it. She dumped all of it into a paper sack, trying not to let the bag rustle too loudly.

As she worked, Alex kept glancing over her shoulder, half expecting to see someone watch-

ing her. She felt like a burgler in her own house!

After dropping a handful of cookies into the sack, Alex carried it carefully over to her backpack which was hanging on a hook by the front door. She stuffed her lunch inside her pack, wincing at every rattle it made.

"Whew," Alex sighed, "that's done." Now all she had to do was turn off the lights and go back upstairs to bed. She returned to the kitchen and flipped the light switch. Immediately, the kitchen was filled with shadows. Alex hurried through the dining room and switched off the light. Entering the living room, she stopped by the lighted lamp. This was the hardest light of all to turn off because as soon as she did the entire house would plunge into darkness.

It's amazing how one light can make you feel so safe, she thought as she stood by the lamp. *I know that when I turn off this lamp, I'll still be in my living room but it won't feel like my living room because it'll be dark and spooky. I wish I had a lamp I could carry around all the time. Then I wouldn't be afraid of dark houses or dark janitor's closets.*

Alex moved so that she was as close to the stairway as possible but still able to reach the lamp. She tried to measure with her eyes how many steps she'd have to take to go from the lamp to the stairs. She then quickly switched off the lamp.

After stumbling to the dark stairway, Alex climbed rapidly. She didn't bother about squeaky steps this time. All she cared about was getting to her bedroom as fast as she could.

When she reached the top of the stairs, she scurried into her room and leaped on her bed.

Brussels sprouts! She had done it!

Morning came too quickly for Alex. It seemed that she had just fallen asleep again when she felt someone pulling at her arm.

"Alex! Wake up! Your alarm didn't go off this morning and it's late." Her mother's voice cut through the dark blanket of sleep.

Alex tried opening her eyes. They didn't want to open. The sunlight from the window was too bright. She squinted at Mother.

"Alex, Honey, you need to get up and get going," her mother told her. "I thought you were already up or I would have come in here sooner. You must have forgotten to set your alarm. Come on, hop out of bed."

Alex did not exactly "hop" out of bed. She kind of rolled, slid, and fell out of bed.

"Get some clothes on and run downstairs," ordered Mother. "Your breakfast is already on the table."

When Alex got downstairs she found bacon and eggs waiting for her on the kitchen table. Her mother and sister were standing in the kitchen. Mother was pointing at the kitchen counter and staring at her sister. Barbara, with her hands on her hips, was staring back at Mother.

"Barbara, you must have forgotten to clean up the counter after you made your lunch last night," accused Mother.

"Mom, I told you. I remember wiping the counter after I made my lunch," insisted Barbara.

"Well, you certainly didn't do a very good job. There are crumbs all over, and look at this knife. It's stuck to the counter with peanut butter!"

"I did make a peanut butter sandwich," Barbara admitted, "but I'm sure I didn't leave the knife stuck to the counter."

"If you didn't, then who did?" asked Mother. "Nobody else made a peanut butter sandwich last night."

Alex choked on her eggs. She was the one who had left the knife stuck to the counter after making her sandwich last night. Now, Miss Mushy was getting the blame. She guiltily watched as Barbara shrugged her shoulders and began cleaning the knife and wiping the crumbs and clumps of peanut butter and jelly off the top of the counter.

As they walked to school together, Alex told Janie how she had sneaked downstairs and made her lunch at midnight.

"Wow, Alex, weren't you scared?" Janie asked.

"Yeah, some," Alex admitted. She kicked a rock, sending it flying down the hill. "You know, Janie, I've been thinking. I've been doing some pretty bad things, like hiding in the janitor's closet and making lunch in the middle of the night, and . . . well, none of it would have happened if we hadn't spent the extra five dollars at the carnival."

"Yeah," Janie agreed.

"I wish we hadn't spent it," sighed Alex.

"Me, too," said Janie.

When Alex's class lined up for its usual lunchtime march to the cafeteria, Alex happily clutched her sack lunch. No janitor's closet today, she sighed in relief. There was one thing she'd forgotten—milk money. Oh, well, she'd have to do without a drink.

When Alex entered the noisy cafeteria, she

hurried to a seat beside Janie. "Boy, am I glad you brought your lunch today, Alex," exclaimed Janie. "I'd hate to think of you spending two days in a row inside that—"

"Shhhhh!" Alex clapped her hand over her friend's mouth. She frowned at Janie and then motioned toward some boys who had sat down at the end of their table. Eddie Thompson was one of them. If Eddie heard about Alex hiding in the janitor's closet, he'd tell Mrs. Tuttle just to get Alex in trouble. He was already angry with Alex for getting the largest and fastest hermit crab in the class. Could she help it if she'd drawn its number out of Mrs. Tuttle's hat the day they were making terrariums?

"Mmmmhhppff!" mumbled Janie. She was trying to remind Alex to take her hand off her mouth. The girls around them giggled. Alex quickly lowered her hand.

"Did you have to do that, Alex?" complained Janie.

"I didn't want the boys to hear you," Alex explained. "We all have to be careful and not let anybody know what I did yesterday or I'll be in big trouble," she told all the girls at the table.

The girls agreed to keep their secret and soon were talking and laughing about other matters. Alex found a way to eat her lunch without getting too thirsty. She would eat a bite of apple after every bite of peanut butter sandwich. That way the juicy apple kept her teeth from sticking together.

"Ouch!" Alex cried suddenly. Something had hit her on the nose! Whatever it was bounced onto the table. Alex peered at what looked like a mushy grape.

"HEY! HOW 'BOUT ANOTHER EYEBALL?" Sinister laughter exploded from the boys' end of the table. Another round object was flipped from a spoon. It hurtled through the air and splashed into Janie's soup.

"YEEACK!" screeched Janie as drops of tomato soup splattered all over her white blouse.

"CUT THAT OUT, EDDIE THOMPSON!" shouted Alex. She quickly ducked under the table as she saw several boys loading their spoons.

SMACK! SPLAT! SMACK! SPLAT! SMACK! SPLAT!

"EEEEEK!" the girls screamed. They all quickly joined Alex under the table as a shower of "eyeballs" splashed around them.

"EYEBALLS! FROGS' EYEBALLS!" roared the boys.

"CHILDREN! WHAT'S GOING ON HERE?" a voice cut through the uproar. They all knew that voice—Mrs. Tuttle.

Upon hearing her teacher's voice, Alex crawled out from under the table. Her foot squished something soft. She jumped back. "Don't be ridiculous," she told herself. "Those aren't eyeballs. They're only grapes." Just the same, Alex was careful where she put her feet.

"You boys will use your recess to clean up this mess!" ordered Mrs. Tuttle. "Girls, pick up the rest of your lunches and move to a clean table."

The girls hurried to obey. The table was a disaster. Smashed grapes covered it. Some of the drinks and soup had been spilled when the girls had scrambled under the table.

Mrs. Tuttle sat down beside Eddie. Alex stole a peek at the boys. They were staring at their plates and looking miserable.

As soon as Alex and her friends were settled at another table, they began to giggle. Those boys! Wouldn't they ever learn to behave? The girls happily finished their lunches and skipped out to the playground for recess.

CHAPTER 5

Treasure Hunting

That evening after dinner, Father, Mother, Barbara, Alex, and Rudy gathered in the family room. It was Tuesday, and every Tuesday evening the family joined together for what they called Treasure Hunting. Father or Mother would read a story from the Bible and then talk about it. As the family discussed the story, they would discover God's messages in the story. Those messages were the treasure. They would see how the treasure could help them in their own lives.

Alex loved Treasure Hunting. The stories were fascinating, and it amazed her to think that they were true. "Things must have been a lot more exciting back then," she told herself. "Today nobody gets thrown into a lions' den like Daniel

or lives inside a whale like Jonah or kills a giant with a slingshot like David. Brussels sprouts! We don't even have any giants around here!"

As much as Alex liked to hear the Bible stories, she liked even more having her family close around her. It reminded her that her family would always be available whenever she needed them. She could feel God's love surrounding and protecting them all.

"All righty, buccaneers, hoist the sail! Raise the anchor! Climb the crow's nest! We're off to search for treasure!" Father's eyes rolled as he twirled the ends of an imaginary mustache. On his head was a magnificent sea captain's hat, a bright red plume stuck in its band. Mother had made the hat for him several years ago when he had dressed as Christopher Columbus for a costume party.

Seeing Father in that hat always made Alex and Rudy giggle. "Look alive or you'll be swabbing the deck!" he told them.

"What are we going to read tonight?" Barbara asked.

"We're not going to read anything tonight," Father announced. He held up his hands as the children began to protest. "I'm going to ask you a question. I want to see if you can answer the question by remembering the stories we already have read."

"What's the question?" Alex immediately wanted to know.

"I was just getting to that, Firecracker. Can you remember any Bible stories in which a person obeyed God?"

"Easy!" cried Alex. "How 'bout Moses?"

"Good. Tell us how Moses obeyed God."

"Are you kidding?" Alex exclaimed. "There were lots of ways he obeyed God. He went to Egypt and told Pharaoh to let the Israelites go; he had all the Israelites put blood over their doors so the Angel of Death would pass over their houses; and he stretched his staff over the sea so that the sea opened up. God told him to do all that stuff."

"That's right, Firecracker! I'm glad to see you've been paying attention to my reading," teased Father.

"Oh, Dad," Alex sighed.

"Would you say that good things happened because Moses obeyed God?" Father asked Alex.

"Sure," she answered. "The Israelites got away from Pharaoh and didn't have to be slaves anymore."

"Very good," her father praised her. "Who else can think of someone who obeyed God?"

"I can," Barbara said. "Shadrach, Meshach, and Abednego obeyed God's commandment not to worship any idols. When King Nebuchadnezzar asked them to worship a gold statue, they wouldn't do it."

"Right," Father agreed, "and what happened to them?"

"Well, they did get thrown into a furnace, but God protected them. When they came out without any burns, the king saw how powerful God was, and no one had to worship the gold statue anymore."

All the time that Barbara was speaking, Rudy bounced up and down on the sofa, his eyes sparkling. As soon as she finished, he popped up from his seat.

"I know one! I know one!" he cried.

"Who?" Father asked him.

"Noah," Rudy proudly announced.

"How did Noah obey God?" asked Father.

"He built the ark when God told him to," Rudy told him.

"And what happened after he built the ark?"

"Well, a big flood came and drowned all the people except Noah and his family and the animals," answered Rudy.

"Very good, Steamroller," Father winked at Rudy. "You've all thought of good examples and we've seen good things happen when people obey God. Now . . ."

"Wait a minute," Mother interrupted. "Don't I get a turn?"

"Oh, of course. Excuse me," replied Father. He made a low bow to Mother. They all laughed.

"I'm thinking of Jesus," said Mother. "He obeyed God and died on the cross for us so that God would forgive our sins and give us eternal life."

"Right. I'm certainly glad Jesus obeyed God," Father exclaimed.

"Me, too," cried Alex. "Now we can live forever with Him." Everybody nodded their heads in agreement.

"I have another question for you," said Father. "Who can think of someone who didn't obey God?"

"Oh, I know," Barbara exclaimed. "Adam and Eve."

Father looked at Barbara. "What happened because Adam and Eve did not obey God?"

"Very funny, Dad," replied Barbara. "We all know what happened in that story. You know, evil came into the world, and that's why the world's in such a big mess now."

"I have to agree with that," said Father. "Adam and Eve listened to Satan instead of to God. They ate an apple that God told them not to eat. They disobeyed God. Did you know that to disobey God is a sin? Look what happened to the world when Adam and Eve disobeyed.

"Yes, Firecracker? I can see you're bursting to tell us about someone else," Father chuckled.

"Jonah!" shouted Alex. "God told him to go to, uh, some city. . . ."

"Nineveh," Mother helped her.

"Oh, yeah, Nineveh," Alex continued, "and Jonah didn't want to go so he got on a ship to go somewhere else. Then God sent a huge storm and the men on the ship threw Jonah overboard and a big fish swallowed him!"

"Do you remember how long Jonah stayed inside that fish, Firecracker?" asked Father.

"Three days and three nights," Alex answered.

"Jonah certainly had a rough time when he disobeyed God, didn't he?" added Father. "How about you, Steamroller? Can you think of anyone who did not obey God?''

Rudy rolled his eyes. He was thinking hard. Barbara leaned over to him and whispered something in his ear.

''Oh, yeah,'' he cried. ''That lady! That lady that turned to salt.''

Father and Mother smiled at each other. Alex and Barbara giggled. ''Do you mean Lot's wife?'' Father asked Rudy.

''Yeah, Lot's wife. She looked back at the city that was burning. The angels had told her not to, but she did anyway, and she was turned into a big high, oh, you know . . .'' Rudy couldn't think of the word. He looked to Father for help.

''A pillar,'' Father prompted him.

''Yeah, a pillar. She turned into a pillar of salt.'' Rudy pointed at his mother. ''Mom, if we ever have to leave our house 'cuz it's on fire, don't look back! Just don't look back!''

Everybody howled with laughter. Rudy looked confused. He was serious. He did not want his mother turned into a pillar of salt.

''Don't worry, Rudy,'' soothed Mother, as she put her arms around him. ''If any angels tell me not to look back, I won't look back. I promise.''

Father smiled and said, ''We have seen good things that happen when people obey God and bad things that happen when people don't obey God. God wants us to obey Him, but like everything else, we have to learn how to obey. Sometimes that can be hard work. So God gave us certain people on earth that we must obey to help us learn obedience. Who do you think those people are?''

''We have to obey the police,'' suggested Barbara.

''That's right. Anybody else?'' Father asked.

''Teachers,'' called Alex.

''Yeah, teachers!'' agreed Rudy. He folded his arms across his chest and wrinkled his nose.

''Teachers and police are good answers,'' agreed Father, ''but I'm thinking of two special people that God gives to children to teach them how to obey.''

''Oh,'' said Barbara, nodding her head, ''you mean our parents!''

''Ohhhhhh,'' echoed Alex and Rudy. Rudy remembered Barbara's world map he had almost ruined and Alex remembered the five dollars she shouldn't have spent at the carnival.

"Well, goodness, you two," their mother laughed. "You look like you expect us to tell you to jump off a bridge or something!"

Father chuckled. "Obeying your parents isn't so bad. God says in the Bible, 'Children, obey your parents in the Lord, for this is right.' So you see, by obeying your parents, you are also obeying God. And what happens when we obey God?"

"Good things!" they all shouted together.

CHAPTER 6

The Valley of the Shadow of Death

Alex awoke the next morning with the sun streaming through her bedroom window. She stretched, then suddenly rose straight up in bed. Her alarm! It hadn't awakened her at midnight!

Alex checked the clock on her radio. Yes, the alarm was set at 12. Why didn't it go off?

Her mother appeared in the doorway. "Oh, you're awake," she said. "Did your alarm go off?"

"No, I just woke up on my own," yawned Alex.

"Well, I know why it hasn't gone off these last two mornings," declared Mother. "Somehow it was set wrong. The goofy thing went off at midnight last night. I had to come in here and turn it off. I'm surprised you slept through all that racket."

After Mother left the room, Alex sat on the edge of her bed and stared at the floor. Part of her wanted to tell her mother what had really happened to the alarm and part of her didn't. She knew that if her mother asked if she'd set the alarm at midnight, she would have to tell her the truth. There had been a time, not long ago, that Alex had found herself in trouble because of several lies she had told. Since that time, she had promised herself and the Lord that she would never tell a lie again.

"Brussels sprouts," Alex told herself. "Mom doesn't even suspect that I set the alarm for midnight. She trusts me not to do things like that. I wonder what she'd think if she knew that I sneaked downstairs in the middle of the night or that I hid in the janitor's closet or that I spent that five dollars at the carnival? If she knew all that, she'd probably never trust me again!"

Alex began pulling on her clothes. She could hear her father singing in the shower. "At least he sounds happy." she grumbled. "Guess it's no lunch and the janitor's closet for me today. It's awful sitting in the dark by myself! Well, I'll just say the 23rd Psalm again. I wonder if I should ask Dad about the valley of the shadow of death?''

Just then the bathroom door opened.

''Dad?'' Alex called.

Her father, dressed in his bathrobe, stuck his head in her doorway. ''Good morning, Firecracker.''

''Dad, I've been wondering about the 23rd Psalm,'' began Alex.

''At six thirty in the morning?'' her father exclaimed.

''Yeah,'' Alex replied with a shrug of her shoulders. ''You see there's a part of it that I don't like to say.''

Father walked over to Alex's bed and sat down beside her. ''What part is that, Firecracker?''

''The scary part,'' Alex answered quickly.

''The scary part?'' asked Father, puzzled.

''Yeah, you know,'' Alex exclaimed, ''the valley of the shadow of death!''

''Oh,'' Father's eyes twinkled. ''I remember a time when that was the scary part for me, too.''

He put his arm around Alex and hugged her close to him.

"You know, Firecracker, sometimes we feel afraid. Maybe we are even in danger. Or perhaps we are very worried about something. I call those troubled times the 'valleys.' "

"You mean like the valley of the shadow of death?" Alex interrupted.

"Exactly," Father replied. "We all have valleys in our lives. But no matter how dark those valleys may seem, we can go through them without fear by trusting Jesus to guide us.

"The Bible tells us that Jesus is our Shepherd and we are His sheep. What does a shepherd do for his sheep?"

"Well, he walks with them," replied Alex.

"Right," agreed Father, "and what else does he do for his sheep?"

"He watches them," Alex answered again.

"He walks with them and watches them to keep them from harm," Father nodded. "A shepherd scares off enemies that try to attack his sheep, and he makes sure that his sheep stay on the right path. That's what Jesus does for us, too. He scares off our enemies and keeps us on the right path through the valleys in our lives."

"Why do we have to go through those creepy valleys anyway?" wondered Alex.

"To get to the top of the mountain, of course," Father grinned at Alex.

"Huh? What do you mean? What mountain?" asked Alex.

"Every spring," Father told her, "a shepherd leads his sheep to higher ground. He wants to get them to the mountaintop to their summer fields of grass. The easiest way to climb a mountain is to go through the valleys along the mountain's slope."

"But what does that have to do with us?" Alex was puzzled. "We aren't climbing any mountain!"

"Oh, but indeed we are, Firecracker," Father told her. "We are climbing the mountain of faith. Every time we allow Jesus, our Shepherd, to lead us through the valleys, we increase our trust in Him. Just like a flock of sheep has to depend on its shepherd to get them through the valleys, so we have to depend on our Shepherd. That builds faith and we climb higher up the faith mountain."

"Brussels sprouts," Alex cried. "That almost makes me want to go through more valleys!"

Father laughed. "This may sound strange, Firecracker, but the more valleys we go through, the stronger we get and the higher up the mountain we climb."

A sudden loud voice broke into their conversation. "WHAT ARE YOU TWO DOING?" Mother stood in the doorway, hands on her hips, staring in amazement at Father and Alex.

"Do you know what time it is?" Mother went on. "You're both going to be late! Neither one of you is dressed and I already have breakfast on the table." Mother tapped her foot in pretend anger.

"We were having a very important conversation," Father explained to Mother. He winked at Alex and hurried out of the room.

Alex rushed around her room, hurriedly grabbing her shoes and socks. She was so glad that she had talked with her father. She felt much better about having to sit in the janitor's closet today. She would go through that valley with her Shepherd!

The rest of the morning went quickly—too quickly—and soon Alex found herself lining up with her class for lunch. Lorraine gave Alex a sympathetic look as she stepped behind Lorraine at the end of the line. Lorraine was always the last one in line. She was too shy to move ahead of anyone else.

Alex felt her knees shake as she followed the line down the hallway. Could she escape her teacher's keen eyes again and duck into the janitor's closet without being noticed?

As the line moved past the closet door, Alex glanced at Mrs. Tuttle. Her teacher was not looking. Alex quietly sidestepped to the door and whisked inside.

Darkness covered her. "I will not be afraid," she told herself. "Yea, though I walk through the valley of the shadow of death, I will fear no evil: for thou art with me; thy rod and thy staff they comfort me!"

As Alex repeated the words over and over, she began to imagine a shaded mountain valley with green grass and a beautiful mountain stream running through it. The picture of the valley brought Alex a feeling of calmness and peace. In fact, she felt so peaceful that she decided to step farther into the darkness and explore the closet.

Alex took a few careful steps deeper into the closet and slowly stretched her arms out on both sides. She felt nothing. Keeping her arms extended, Alex stepped farther and farther into the closet. Suddenly, her left arm brushed against something. It felt like a pole. Probably nothing but an old broom, Alex decided. She tried to grab it. It slipped sideways and knocked into something beside it. That "something" slipped sideways and hit something else. Before Alex knew it, everything on the left side of the closet was falling noisily to the floor! Something crashed into Alex. She lost her balance and tumbled over.

CHAPTER 7

Crash!
Crack!
Smash!
Shatter!

Alex hit the floor hard. Thuds, clangs, and bangs sounded everywhere. It seemed like the entire closet was collapsing around her! Something soft and squishy and rather damp flopped across her face.

"YEEACK!" Alex pulled what felt like a mop off of her face and slung it sideways. BANG! It hit the wall.

Alex didn't make another move. She lay on the floor of the closet listening for footsteps. Surely everyone in the school building had heard the uproar.

Twenty-five . . . fifty . . . one hundred seconds and no footsteps. Alex counted another one hundred seconds. All was quiet. She began to relax.

"Tap! Tap! Tap!"

What was that?

"Tap! Tap! Tap!"

It sounded like someone tapping on the door! Alex froze.

"Alex? A-l-e-x?" called a soft voice. Was that Janie?

"Alex! Hurry up and open the door!" The voice demanded. It was Janie's voice.

Alex sprang off the floor and started for the door. BANG! CRASH! "OUCH!" She tripped over something. Alex rubbed her knee. Hobbling to the door, she felt for the doorknob and opened the door cautiously, just a crack.

"Janie?"

"Alex? What took you so long? Here, I brought you something. Hold out your hands."

With her eyes wide open in amazement, Alex shoved her arms out the door. Janie dropped something warm into her hands, turned, and fled down the hall.

Alex looked down. A hot dog! Janie had brought her a hot dog. Brussels sprouts!

Alex grinned and quickly backed into the closet, closing the door behind her. She ate the hot

dog in three big bites.

"RRRIIINNNGGG!" The loud blast of the school bell made Alex jump and cover her ears.

Once again, Alex waited for her teacher and her class to pass by the crack in the closet door. Once again, she crept with shaky legs behind Lorraine at the end of the line. Once again, she passed by a suspicious-looking Mrs. Tuttle at the door to the playground.

"Alex?" her teacher held out a hand. "I don't remember seeing you in the lunchroom."

Alex skidded to a stop. Her mouth opened

wide. She stared at her teacher, not knowing what to say. Quite by accident, she must have looked innocent to Mrs. Tuttle. Her teacher shrugged her shoulders and said, "I must have just missed seeing you. Go on out to recess."

Alex stumbled out the door to her waiting friends. "I better not hide in that closet any-more," she told them. "Mrs. Tuttle almost caught me!"

Late that afternoon, Alex trudged up the hill to her house. She had just come from softball prac-tice. Usually softball practice filled her with energy, but today she was tired. Alex decided that was because she was so hungry.

When Alex reached home, she collapsed on her back on the top step of the front porch. Back-pack, books, and softball mitt tumbled down the steps where she dropped them.

"Alex's home! Come on!" Two pair of eager feet clattered up the driveway, up the walk, up the steps, and with a plop, landed on either side of Alex's head. Alex did not have to open her eyes to know who belonged to those feet.

"Goblin," she groaned, "I am too tired."

"Aw, Alex, come on," pleaded Rudy.

"Please, Alex," begged another voice.

Alex squinted at Rudy and his best friend, Jason. Jason lived next door to Alex and Rudy. Alex liked Jason. He was easier to get along with than her brother. Alex often wondered if that was because his father was a minister. Maybe spending so much time at church made Jason a neat kid.

Both boys bent over Alex and peered at her face. They wore such pitiful looks on their faces that Alex chuckled.

"Oh, she's just teasing us, Jason," Rudy said in relief.

"No, I'm not, Goblin," insisted Alex. "I'm too hot and tired and hungry and thirsty to practice softball with you."

Rudy frowned at Jason. He and Jason needed Alex's help. They were going to start playing Little League ball next week for the first time.

Suddenly, Rudy's face brightened. "Wait right here, Alex," he ordered. "Don't go away!"

Rudy banged open the front door and disappeared into the house. In a few moments he returned hugging a banana, a chocolate cupcake, and a tall glass of ice water in his arms.

"There!" Rudy proudly plopped the goodies down beside Alex. "That'll make you feel better."

Alex stared at her brother in surprise. There were times when she actually liked the little brat. This was one of those times.

"Thanks, Goblin," Alex muttered, grabbing the ice water and gulping down half of it. She quickly wolfed down the banana. She ate the cupcake slowly to make it last as long as possible. After drinking the rest of the ice water, Alex had to admit she did feel better.

The boys sat on the step beside her, anxiously watching her every move. Finally, Rudy could stand it no longer. "Well," he cried. "Do you feel like playing now?"

Alex turned her head very slowly and looked at her brother. She teased him by not answering right away. Suddenly, she grabbed her softball mitt off the bottom step and ran out into the middle of the yard.

"BATTER UP!" she hollered.

Rudy and Jason shouted with glee and ran with Alex to the backyard. Their own small softball diamond sat in the farthest corner of the yard, its base paths worn smooth by active feet. The V of the fence corner served as the backstop. The pitcher's mound had been raised by many wagon loads of dirt.

Alex stood on her own pitcher's mound. This was a favorite place. She loved to pitch. She was the star pitcher for her own team, the Tornadoes.

Jason batted first.

"Choke up on the bat more, Jason!" Alex called.

Jason quickly moved his hands up on the bat. He always followed Alex's advice. Alex was the best ballplayer he knew.

Alex threw some pitches. Jason missed more than he hit.

"Put your hands together, Jason!

"Watch the ball, Jason!"

"My turn!" Rudy announced loudly. He was tired of fielding.

"Just a minute! Just a minute!" Alex hollered. She quickly strode to the plate and grabbed the bat out of Jason's hands.

"Now, watch," she told Rudy and Jason. "See, I put my feet here like this—not too close and not too far from the plate. Then, I bring my left foot close to my right foot so when the ball comes in, I can step sideways into the pitch. That gives me more power."

Jason and Rudy watched intently as Alex demonstrated her batting position. Alex was extremely serious when it came to softball. It was a very important activity in her life.

"When you hold a bat, keep your hands together." Alex held the bat over her shoulder. "Choke up on the bat if it feels too long or heavy. The higher you choke up on it, the faster you can swing!" Alex swung the bat a few times.

"When you swing a bat," Alex continued, "swing it level and swing it smooth. Don't try to kill the ball, just try to meet the ball with the bat. Never take your eyes off the ball!" She stared at the boys to see if they understood. They nodded their heads.

"Let me try!" cried Rudy.

Alex handed him the bat with an I-hope-you-paid-attention look on her face.

Rudy took some time getting ready to swing. He was trying to imitate Alex's every example. He took a few practice swings.

"Ready?" Alex called from the mound. Rudy nodded. His face was set with a determined look. Alex went into her windup. She held the ball in her right hand, drew both hands up to her chest, blew a bubble with her gum, leaned to the right, threw her right arm in two circles behind her and her left leg in front of her, popped the bubble, bent her left knee, leaned forward, and released the ball.

It flew straight over home plate.

"CRACK!" went Rudy's bat.

The ball soared up, up, higher and higher, over Alex's head, over Jason's head, and over the fence! The children watched it excitedly. Rudy hopped about in joy. He had hit the ball well!

All in an instant, the happy looks on the children's faces turned to looks of horror. The ball was heading straight into the glass porch at the back of Jason's house!

Jason covered his eyes. Rudy covered his ears.

Alex pointed at the ball, opened her mouth, but no sound came out.

"CRASH! CRACK! SMASH! SHATTER!" The noise was terrible. Pieces of glass flew as one enormous pane crunched to the ground!

For a moment, none of them could move. Then, panic gripped the children. Alex, Rudy, and Jason raced out of the backyard and into the front yard, dropping behind some bushes to hide.

CHAPTER 8

Listen to My Heart?

Alex, Rudy, and Jason crouched low behind a row of bushes in Alex's front yard. Peeking through the branches, they saw Jason's mother run to her backyard. They heard her cries of alarm as she discovered the now-ruined glass porch. The children held their breath as they heard Alex's mother join Jason's mother in the backyard. A few minutes later both mothers began calling their children's names.

"Come on, Rudy! Mom's calling us! We have to go!" Alex began crawling out of the bushes, dragging Rudy behind her.

"Do we have to, Alex?" Rudy clung to a branch, making it impossible for Alex to pull him any further.

Alex looked at her brother. "What else are we going to do? Spend the night here in the bushes?

We shouldn't have run away in the first place. We should have stayed there and explained what happened."

"ALEX! RUDY!" Their mother sounded angry.

"JASON!" shouted his mother.

"Alex is right, Rudy. We better go!" Jason scrambled out of the bushes.

"You're not the one who smashed in your porch, Jason," Rudy replied hotly. "I'm the one who'll get in all the trouble!"

"Look, it wasn't your fault," Alex told Rudy.

"I mean, it wasn't like you broke the porch on purpose. We'll go with you, and I'll do the talking, okay?"

"Oh, okay," grumbled Rudy. He slowly followed Alex out of the bushes.

Just then a car pulled into the driveway. It was Father coming home from work.

"Oh, no!" Rudy exclaimed. Alex held onto his hand tightly to keep him from diving back under the bushes.

As Father was getting out of his car, another car pulled into Jason's driveway. It was Jason's father.

Alex felt Jason quickly grab her other hand. Rudy's lips began to quiver as tears streamed down his face. Alex felt frightened, too. Trying to explain a broken porch to two angry mothers was hard enough, but explaining it to two angry mothers and two angry fathers was worse!

At that instant, the mothers strode around the corner of the house and found their children. "ALEX! RUDY! JASON!"

"What's going on?" Father asked as he gazed at three frightened children and two upset mothers. Jason's father joined the group.

"Follow us!" both mothers commanded. They led the way to Jason's backyard. Father, Jason's father, Jason, Alex, and Rudy walked behind them.

"Oh, no!" Father cried, as he saw the damaged porch.

"What happened?" exclaimed Jason's father.

"That's what I'd like to know. We found a softball in the middle of the broken glass!" Mother folded her arms across her chest and stared at the three children.

No one said anything for a long minute. Alex knew it was up to her to start talking, but there was a big lump in her throat. She cleared her throat several times.

"Well, see, uh," she choked. "I was helping Rudy and Jason with their batting and, well, Rudy hit the ball real good and it sorta flew into the porch. He didn't mean to do it!"

When she finished speaking, Alex was surprised to see a grin spreading across her father's face. He couldn't keep back his chuckles. Mother glared at him.

"I'm sorry, I can't help it!" laughed Father. "I remember doing the same thing when I was a boy, only I didn't break a glass porch. I slugged one through the school window. Hit old man Wilcox as he stood in front of the blackboard teaching sixth-grade math. Boy, did he ever get mad!"

"HA, HA, HA, HA!" roared Jason's father. "I did better'n that! The first ball I hit through a window flew into a grocery store. Landed in a big barrel full of pickles. Pickle juice ran through those aisles!"

The two men laughed hilariously at each other. The mothers looked at each other and shook their heads. The children began to smile. Things didn't seem as bad now.

When the laughter died down, Mother said to the children, "I understand how it happened, but after you broke the glass, you should not have run away. Even though you did not mean to break the glass, you still broke it. When something bad happens because of something you do, you need to admit it and try to do whatever you can to make it right again."

"I'm sorry," Alex apologized. "I know it was wrong for us to run and hide in the bushes. Even when I was running away, I knew it was wrong. I couldn't stop myself. I was too scared."

"I understand," replied Mother, smiling down at her.

"So do I," Jason's father added. He squatted down in front of the three children. "Alex said something that interests me," he told them. "She said that she knew she should not have run away, but she did so anyway because she was afraid. What about you, Jason and Rudy? Did you think it was right to run after you broke the glass?"

"No," Jason and Rudy answered together.

"Let me ask you another question," said Jason's father. "You usually know when you are doing something good, don't you?"

"Yes," the children agreed.

"And, you usually know when you are doing something bad, don't you?"

The children nodded their heads.

Jason's father smiled at the children. "That is your heart speaking to you," he told them.

They looked at him with astonished faces. He

laughed. "You see, God wants us to do good, so He gave each one of us the ability to know what is right and what is wrong. He planted that knowledge deep down in our hearts.

"You need to listen to your heart and do what it tells you is the right thing to do even when you're afraid. Don't let the fear rob you of the joy that you get from doing the right thing."

As Jason's father talked, Alex felt a kind of "jump" inside of her. Was that her heart telling her to listen to it? Something had been telling her that hiding in the janitor's closet was wrong. So was sneaking downstairs at midnight to make her lunch. Other bad things had happened too—like her sister being blamed for the peanut butter mess in the kitchen. And even Alex's being too tired and hungry to play well at softball practice. It all came from spending that five dollars at the carnival. She wished she had obeyed her mother and her heart!

"Well," her father's voice broke into her thoughts. "I think you owe Jason's parents an apology." He looked sternly at Alex and Rudy.

"I'm sorry," Alex and Rudy responded.

"Me, too," added Jason.

"Has anyone thought of who is going to pay to get the porch fixed?" Father raised his eyebrows at the children.

"Uh," Alex dug in the dirt with her toe. "I only have a dollar and thirty-seven cents in my bank. I'm sure that's not enough."

"Well, I have two quarters and three nickels and seven pennies," Rudy added proudly.

"How much does that make, Rudy?" chuckled Father.

"Oh, about a dollar," guessed Rudy. The grownups laughed.

"I only have three cents," voiced Jason. "I spent all my money on food for Clementine and Homer." Clementine and Homer were Jason's pet turtles.

"How much does glass cost anyway, Dad?" Jason asked his father. "Do we have enough?"

"Hmm," Jason's father stroked his chin. "With the insurance money, you might have enough." More chuckles came from the grownups.

Insurance! There is that word again, thought

Alex. She remembered her parents had talked about insurance when she had accidently whomped her father's car with a wagon load of rocks. "Insurance must be something parents get when their kids mess up and wreck something," Alex told herself. "Maybe it's a kind of reward for having to put up with clumsy kids."

Alex and Rudy followed their parents inside. It was dinnertime. Alex made sure to help her mother in the kitchen. It was always good to help out parents after you had made them mad. Even Rudy set the table with no complaints.

That night in bed, Alex decided that she was going to listen to her heart, and she was going to do what her heart told her to do. After all, God was the Maker of her heart. If she listened to it, she would really be listening to Him.

She did not set her alarm for midnight. It was wrong to sneak downstairs at midnight. What about hiding in the janitor's closet? Her heart told her that was also wrong. What else could she do? Tell her parents everything? Not tonight! Not after breaking a glass porch.

Alex flopped over to her stomach and wiggled

into her favorite sleeping position. She was too tired to think about it tonight. She would think about it tomorrow. She hugged her stuffed Garfield tightly and fell fast asleep.

CHAPTER 9

Caught at Last

The next morning, Alex did not have much time to worry about lunch. Mrs. Tuttle kept the class busy with reading and math and spelling. She hurried the class through their lessons. A speaker was going to visit them later that morning. The speaker's name was Mrs. Popham, and she was going to talk about Kansas history.

Alex was tired of hearing about her state's history. If one more person told her about sod houses and covered wagons and the Santa Fe Trail, Alex thought she just might scream. She hoped Mrs. Popham would not bring them a sunflower to color. If one more person gave her a sunflower to color, Alex was going to color it purple.

When Mrs. Popham entered the classroom, she carried a chart under her left arm. On the chart, Alex could see a curvy dotted line marked "Santa Fe Trail." Alex quickly covered her mouth to stop any screams that might come out of it. Mrs. Popham also balanced a small sod house and covered wagon in her hands.

Mrs. Popham was a tiny, silver-haired lady who looked like she might really have lived in the pioneer days. She said she was going to tell the class about how her great-great-grandmother traveled in a covered wagon many hundreds of miles, and how her great-great-grandmother helped to build a sod house, and how her great-great-grandmother lived in that sod house for years and years.

The class listened to Mrs. Popham tell of hardships and troubles experienced while journeying west. About the time in Mrs. Popham's story when the poor, tired oxen pulled the covered wagon out of the third muddy river, Alex felt a tap on her shoulder.

"Hey, Alex! Look!" whispered Chrissy, who sat behind her.

Alex turned around and almost shouted out loud. Eddie Thompson had his hand in one of the hermit crab terrariums and was slowly pulling out a crab! He set it on the floor and tapped his foot behind it. The hermit crab began a frightened crawl toward the front of the classroom.

That dumb Eddie Thompson! Of course, he had picked Alex's terrarium and that was her crab, Sandpan, crawling on the floor. Eddie Thompson had always been jealous of Sandpan because he was the biggest and fastest hermit crab in the class.

Sandpan! Poor Sandpan! The crab would stop and try to hide in his shell, but there was always some boy nearby to tap a foot behind him and make him crawl on.

All the children watched Sandpan out of the corners of their eyes. A few giggles sounded now and then, but Mrs. Popham thought the class was laughing at the funny parts of her story and she would laugh with them. Mrs. Tuttle kept glancing at the children with puzzled looks, but because Sandpan was too little for her to notice on the classroom floor, the teacher did not discover the true reason for their laughter.

Alex almost wished Mrs. Tuttle would see Sandpan. She'd rather have her teacher angry than have something horrible happen to her hermit crab. What if he got squished or something? Alex had taken good care of Sandpan. He was getting used to her touch and didn't even hide in his shell anymore when she picked him up. Now these stupid boys were making him afraid again and ruining everything!

Should she get up and rescue Sandpan? He was almost to the front of the room. Too late. Allen Jacobs, who sat in the front row, snatched up the crab.

Slyly grinning at the other boys, he waited until Mrs. Tuttle was not looking and Mrs. Popham was pointing at her chart. He then quickly placed Sandpan on top of the table where the sod house and covered wagon sat.

Mrs. Popham left her chart and walked over to the table. She was ready to demonstrate how to build a sod house. Sandpan sat a few inches away from the house. He was drawn into his shell. He looked like a plain ordinary seashell.

"Oh, my goodness!" Mrs. Popham exclaimed. "Whatever is a seashell doing here?"

At that moment, several things happened at once: Mrs. Popham picked up the shell. Sandpan peeked out of the shell. Alex jumped out of her chair. Mrs. Popham screamed! Alex ran forward. Mrs. Popham flung the shell away from her! Alex dove over two desks and caught Sandpan in midair!

"Alexandria Brackenbury!" exclaimed Mrs. Tuttle.

Alex lay on the floor and clutched Sandpan,

hoping desperately that the crab was all right. "It wasn't my fault," she managed to tell Mrs. Tuttle.

"That's right!" one of the girls shouted. "Eddie Thompson took her crab out of the terrarium!"

"Yeah, and Allen Jacobs put it up on the table!" cried another girl.

Instantly, all the girls in the class began talking at once, loudly explaining to Mrs. Tuttle what had happened.

Mrs. Tuttle held up her hands. Everyone quieted down.

"Eddie Thompson and Allen Jacobs will come with me!" she ordered. "Alex, please put your crab back in its terrarium."

"Oh, let me see if he's okay" wailed Alex. She was almost in tears. Sandpan had completely disappeared into his shell and wouldn't move even when she touched him.

"All right," Mrs. Tuttle sighed, "take him to your desk. I'm sorry, Mrs. Popham, please go on with your talk." The teacher left the room with Eddie Thompson and Allen Jacobs.

Mrs. Popham nervously continued speaking. Alex did not hear one word. She was overjoyed when Sandpan finally decided to take a crawl on her hand.

Mrs. Tuttle soon returned without the two boys. Mrs. Popham finished speaking and passed out a sheet of paper to each child. Alex looked at hers. It was an outline of a giant sunflower!

Alex was looking for her purple crayon when Mrs. Tuttle announced that it was lunchtime. Alex quickly put Sandpan back into his terrarium. She'd forgotten all about lunch in the excitement of the morning. What was she going to do? She knew she wasn't supposed to hide in the janitor's closet anymore. But the only other thing she could do was to tell her teacher that she didn't have any lunch. Her teacher would ask her why she didn't have any lunch. She would have to explain everything to Mrs. Tuttle. It would be easier to hide in the janitor's closet one more time. Alex ran to the back of the line behind Lorraine.

When the class marched passed the janitor's closet, Alex tiptoed sideways and reached for the closet's doorknob. It wouldn't turn. The door was locked! Alex twisted and turned the knob frantically.

A hand suddenly clamped down on Alex's shoulder! "So this is the closet burglar," growled a low voice. Alex twisted around to see Mr. Whitney, the school's janitor, standing over her.

"I'm not a burglar," she squeaked.

"You don't say?" retorted Mr. Whitney. "Well, someone got into my closet yesterday and just about tore it to pieces! Wouldn't have been you, would it?" Mr. Whitney glared at her.

"I didn't mean to tear up your closet. I was only hiding." Alex was terribly afraid. It was all over now. She had been caught!

"Hiding? What were you hiding from?" asked Mr. Whitney.

Alex couldn't answer. She knew if she tried to say one more word, tears would flood her face.

"Well, hmmmpf," Mr. Whitney snorted, "you better talk this over with Mrs. Larson. Come along now."

Mrs. Larson was the school principal. Mr.

Whitney and Alex walked down the hall to her office. They had to pass by the cafeteria. Alex stared straight ahead. She didn't dare look in the cafeteria window. She hoped Mrs. Tuttle wouldn't see her.

"We need to see the principal," Mr. Whitney announced to the office secretary. The secretary gave Mr. Whitney and Alex a surprised look. Alex wished there were a hole she could fall into and disappear.

"I believe Mrs. Larson will be right out," the secretary told them.

A moment later, the principal's door opened. Out stepped Mrs. Larson, Eddie Thompson, and Allen Jacobs. Alex ducked her head and scrunched as close to the wall as she could. She hoped the boys wouldn't notice her.

"Okay, boys, you may go eat lunch now, but report to your teacher at recess time," ordered Mrs. Larson. "She'll make sure you have something to do besides causing mischief."

Both boys turned toward the door. They had to pass by Alex on their way out.

"ALEX!" they cried when they saw her.

Alex didn't answer or look at them. She couldn't. She couldn't look at anyone. Her face reddened and she tried hard to blink back the tears that were already blurring all the colors of the carpet together. She felt like a criminal. For what seemed like forever, Mrs. Larson, Mr. Whitney, the office secretary, Eddie Thompson, and Allen Jacobs stood and stared at her.

CHAPTER 10

Higher Up the Mountain

"WHAT ARE YOU DOING HERE?" hollered Eddie Thompson and Allen Jacobs. They each pointed a finger at Alex.

Alex leaned against the wall of the school office. She was so ashamed. She could hardly stand up.

"That is none of your business," Mrs. Larson told the boys. She sent them out of the office.

"Well, Mr. Whitney, what may I do for you and Alex?" the principal asked.

"Caught this little girl trying to get into my closet," Mr. Whitney reported.

"What?" exclaimed Mrs. Larson.

"Caught her trying to get into my closet," Mr. Whitney repeated. "She's the one that wrecked up the place yesterday."

“Not Alex!” Mrs. Larson cried.

“Afraid so,” mumbled the janitor, rubbing his chin. “Said she was hiding.”

“Hiding?” Mrs. Larson looked confused. “Well, Alex, I think we’d better talk about this. Come on inside my office. Thank you, Mr. Whitney.”

Mr. Whitney left the office, still rubbing his chin. Alex forced her rubbery legs to follow the principal into her office.

“Alex, I can hardly believe this about you,” said Mrs. Larson.

“Me, neither,” mumbled Alex, finally finding her voice. “It’s sorta unbelievable.”

“Oh, dear. Well, suppose you tell me why you were hiding in the janitor’s closet.” Mrs. Larson smiled such a friendly smile that Alex lost some of her fear.

Alex poured out her story to the principal. She told her about the carnival and the five dollars that she shouldn’t have spent and hiding in the janitor’s closet and making her lunch at midnight.

“Goodness, Alex,” Mrs. Larson said when Alex had finished. “It sounds like you’ve been through a few rough days.'' She patted Alex's hand. ''I can tell you feel bad about the whole thing.''

Alex nodded her head. ''I'm sorry about messing up the janitor's closet,'' she gulped.

Mrs. Larson chuckled, ''I think we will have you help Mr. Whitney during one of your recesses tomorrow. There should be some little job that you could help him with. That should make him feel better about having his closet 'wrecked up,' as he puts it.''

Alex nodded again. Help Mr. Whitney? How could she help Mr. Whitney? She wasn't very good at mopping floors.

''I will explain all of this to your teacher, Alex,'' promised Mrs. Larson. ''But you will have to explain it to your parents. I'll call them later and say that you have something to tell them. That way, when you get home, you can tell them about it in your own words.''

Alex sighed. Telling her parents was going to be hard.

''Here's a pass so that you can go eat lunch, Alex. You'll have to eat with the fifth and sixth graders. I'm sure your regular lunch period is over by now. After you eat, you can return to your class.'' Mrs. Larson smiled at her. ''Thank you for telling me what happened, Alex. I think everything will turn out all right.''

When Alex got back to her classroom, she reached the door just as the other children were coming in from recess.

''Alex! Where were you?'' Janie asked.

Alex quickly shushed her. She did not want everyone in the class to know about her visit to the principal. Eddie Thompson and Allen Jacobs grinned wickedly at her. She ignored them. They had nothing to grin at her about. After all, they had just spent their recess with Mrs. Tuttle.

The afternoon pressed on. Alex spent most of it worrying. Had Mrs. Larson called her parents? What did she say to them?

The last bell of the day rang. Alex pulled Janie out the door. She waited until Rudy and Jason were far ahead of them before she told Janie all that had happened. The two girls wondered what Alex's parents would say and do. Alex hoped she wouldn't be grounded for too long.

As soon as her father came home from work, Mother sent Rudy next door to play with Jason. Barbara was at a friend's house. Alex was alone with her parents.

Alex sat nervously on the edge of a chair in the living room. Her father sat down across from her in another chair. Her mother seated herself on the sofa.

"Well, Firecracker," her father broke the silence. "Your principal called today."

"Yes, Mrs. Larson said you had something to tell us," added Mother.

"Oh, uh, yeah," stuttered Alex. She shifted in her chair. She wondered what had happened to her voice. It sounded dry and raspy and kind of far away—not like her own voice at all.

"Just start at the beginning," her mother encouraged her. "Once you get started, it'll be easier."

Alex swallowed hard. "Okay, uh, remember that ten dollars you gave me to take to the carnival?"

Her mother looked surprised but nodded her head.

''And, uh, remember how I was only s'posed to spend five dollars of it?''

Her mother nodded again.

''Well, see, Janie and I were real upset by the haunted house and we used up all our money except the last five dollars and Janie wanted to do the Cake Walk again and I felt bad because she couldn't do it. Well, anyway, I spent all the money!'' Alex ducked her head and waited for her parents to yell.

No one yelled. No one even spoke for a long minute. Then Mother said, ''That means you didn't have any lunch money this week. What did you do for lunches?''

''Uh, hmmph,'' Alex cleared her throat. ''I hid in the janitor's closet at lunch.''

''What?'' exclaimed Mother.

''You hid in the janitor's closet every day this week?'' asked Father in amazement.

''Well, not exactly,'' Alex told him. ''Today I didn't 'cuz I got caught by the janitor, and one day I took my lunch.''

''You took your lunch?'' questioned Mother. ''I don't remember making a lunch for you to take to school this week.''

''You didn't make it, Mom. I made it. I, uh, sorta made it at midnight.'' Alex ducked her head again.

''Midnight!'' both parents cried.

''Yeah, I set my alarm for midnight and came downstairs and made my lunch.''

''That's why your alarm went off at midnight,'' Mother said. She looked at Father and they both sighed.

''And Barbara got blamed for the peanut butter mess the next morning and it was really me that made it,'' Alex added.

''Oh, dear,'' Mother sighed again. ''But, Alex,'' she asked, ''weren't you afraid to go downstairs at midnight?''

''Yes,'' Alex admitted. ''I was afraid to turn off the lamp in the living room. I kept wishing I had a light I could carry around with me everywhere.''

''You do, Firecracker,'' Father said. ''Jesus is your Light, and He goes with you everywhere.''

Alex thought about that for a moment. ''Yeah,'' she said slowly. ''I know He was in the janitor's closet with me. He helped me feel better, especially when I said the 23rd Psalm.''

''The 23rd Psalm!'' exclaimed Father. ''So that's why you asked me about it.''

''Oh, yeah,'' Alex replied. ''It was really dark in the closet and I was sorta scared and the only thing I could think of to say was the 23rd Psalm. But I didn't like that part about the valley of the shadow of death 'cuz I didn't understand about the valleys.''

''Do you understand now?'' Father asked.

''I think so.'' Alex was silent for a few moments. Then she added, ''I think I've been going through a really big valley, but now I'm at the end of it.''

''Why do you say that, Firecracker?'' asked Father.

''Well, because I've learned so much. It sounds funny, but I even feel older.''

''What have you learned, Alex?'' her mother asked.

''Well, now I know how important it is to obey your parents and that when you obey your parents, you're also obeying God. I mean, none of

this would've happened if I'd saved the five dollars like you told me to."

"Hmmmpf!" Father looked surprised. "I talked about obeying God and obeying parents the other night because Rudy had disobeyed us and used Barbara's poster paint. I didn't know that you had so much need for that lesson, Firecracker."

"The Lord knew she needed to hear it," said Mother. "It sounds like He's been guiding you through this whole thing," she told Alex.

"Yeah, and I guess I knew all along that He

wanted me to stop hiding and sneaking around and tell you all about it, but I didn't listen to Him 'cuz I was too scared. Just like yesterday when we broke the glass porch. I was too scared and I ran away." Alex hung her head. "I guess I'm not a very good sheep."

Her parents laughed.

"Not true, Firecracker, not true," boomed Father. "You are just as good a sheep as any of us. We all make mistakes. That's why we need our Shepherd to lead us . . . and to get us out of sticky situations."

"Yeah, He got me out of this one all right," exclaimed Alex. "I just hope that next time something happens, I'll listen to my heart and to my Shepherd."

"You'll get better and better at it," laughed her mother. "You see, Jesus not only leads us through the valleys, but He teaches us as we go. That's what it means to grow up in the Lord. Remember, you said a little while ago that you felt older? You are older. Every time you learn something from the Lord, your faith grows."

"And I climb higher up the mountain!" shouted Alex. Her face shone with excitement. "Brussels sprouts! All this time I've been climbing the faith mountain and I didn't even know it!"

Alex felt sudden tears in her eyes. She looked at her parents and saw tears in their eyes, too. At the same time, she and her father moved to sit by Mother on the sofa. All three hugged each other tightly.

"God is so good," whispered Mother.

Amen.

SHOELACES AND BRUSSELS SPROUTS

One little lie, but BIG trouble!

When Alex lies to her mom about losing her shoelaces, it doesn't seem like a big deal. But how do you replace special baseball laces when you don't have any money and you're not allowed to go to the store alone? A big softball game is coming up, and Alex knows the coach won't let her pitch in shoes without laces—or in cowboy boots!

Every kid gets into the predicaments that Alex does—ones that start out small and mushroom. Readers will learn from Alex's mistakes and understand that they have the same sources of help that she turns to: A God who loves them and wants to help them, and parents who understand.

Other books in the Alex Series . . .

2 *French Fry Forgiveness*—Sometimes making friends is harder than making enemies.

3 *Hot Chocolate Friendship*—Is winning first place as important to Alex as being a friend?

4 *Peanut Butter and Jelly Secrets*—Obeying her parents (even in little things) beats the awful results of disobeying.

NANCY LEVENE, who shares Alex's love of softball, lives with her husband and daughter in Kansas.

FRENCH FRY FORGIVENESS

Two Alexandrias!

Alex (short for Alexandria) expects to make new friends when she joins the swim team—but she doesn't count on meeting *another* Alexandria! How can she make friends with Alexandria, who pushes her into the pool for no reason?

Alex knows she should forgive Alexandria, but that seems impossible! Is there *anything* Alex can do to win Alexandria's friendship?

Every kid gets into the predicaments that Alex does—ones that start out small and mushroom. Readers will learn from Alex's mistakes and understand that they have the same sources of help that she turns to: A God who loves them and wants to help them, and parents who understand.

Other books in the Alex Series . . .

1 *Shoelaces and Brussels Sprouts*—It's always better to tell the truth, as Alex learns the hard way.

3 *Hot Chocolate Friendship*—Is winning first place as important to Alex as being a friend?

4 *Peanut Butter and Jelly Secrets*—Obeying her parents (even in little things) beats the awful results of disobeying.

NANCY LEVENE, who shares Alex's love of softball, lives with her husband and daughter in Kansas.

HOT CHOCOLATE FRIENDSHIP

The worst possible partner!

That's who Alex gets for the biggest project of the school year. She won't have a chance at first place if she has to work with Eric Linden. He's the slowest kid in third grade.

Alex can't understand why he has to be her partner. Is she supposed to share God's love with Eric? Could that be more important than winning first place?

Every kid gets into the predicaments that Alex does—ones that start out small and mushroom. Readers will learn from Alex's mistakes and understand that they have the same sources of help that she turns to: A God who loves them and wants to help them, and parents who understand.

Other books in the Alex Series . . .

1 *Shoelaces and Brussels Sprouts*—It's always better to tell the truth, as Alex learns the hard way.

2 *French Fry Forgiveness*—Sometimes making friends is harder than making enemies.

4 *Peanut Butter and Jelly Secrets*—Obeying her parents (even in little things) beats the awful results of disobeying.

NANCY LEVENE, who shares Alex's love of softball, lives with her husband and daughter in Kansas.

THE KIDS FROM APPLE STREET CHURCH

How did it happen?

Every day brings new excitement in the lives of Mary Jo, Danny, and the other kids from Apple Street Church. Whether it's finding a stolen doll in a coat sleeve, chasing important papers all over the school yard, meeting a famous astronaut, or discovering the real truth about a mysteriously broken leg, the kids write it all in their personal notebooks to God.

Usually diaries are private. But this is your chance to look over the shoulders of The Kids from Apple Street Church as they tell God about their secret thoughts, their problems, and their fun times. It's just like praying, except they are writing to God instead of talking to Him.

Don't miss any of the adventures of The Kids from Apple Street Church!

1. Mary Jo Bennett
2. Danny Petrowski
3. Julie Chang
4. Pug McConnell
5. Becky Garcia
6. Curtis Anderson

ELSPETH CAMPBELL MURPHY has also written the popular God's Word in My Heart and David and I Talk to God series.